D0515713

Yoon
and the
Christmas
Mitten

Helen Recorvits

Pictures by Gabi Swiatkowska

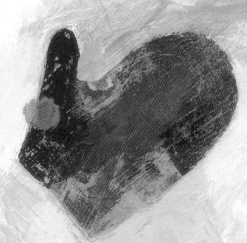

Frances Foster Books

Farrar, Straus and Giroux / New York

My name is Yoon. I came here from Korea, a country far away.

One winter day my teacher in my new American school read my class a story. It was about Mr. Santa Claus, who lived at the North Pole.

"Santa comes on Christmas Eve and brings us presents," the freckle boy told me.

My teacher let me take the Christmas book home, and that night I showed it to my father.

"Look, Father!" I said. "Here is a story about Mr. Santa Claus." I told my father all about the man in the red suit. I showed him the picture of the red-and-white-striped North Pole. I giggled and turned to the page with the sleigh piled high with presents.

My father pushed the book away. "We are Korean. Santa Claus is not our custom."

I hung my head. "But the boys and girls at school say he will visit on Christmas Eve."

"Little Yoon," my mother said, "we are not a Christmas family. Our holiday is New Year's Day. We will visit our friends the Kim family. We will have a fine meal together, and we will wish each other good luck." She smiled. "You can wear your red dress on the celebration day."

I stomped my foot. "I do not like that dress! The collar pinches, and the buttons pop open!" I stomped my foot again.

My mother raised her eyebrows.

"Enough, Yoon!" my father said. "This is not respectful! Go to your room! Go!"

I hugged the Christmas book to my heart. I ran to my room, doing as I was told.

Why did my father not like Mr. Santa Claus? Why did my father not like Christmas?

Later that night I sat on my bed looking at the pictures of the North Pole. My mother came into my room. Quickly I hid the book under my pillow.

"Here, Little Yoon. I saved some for you. Your favorite," she said. She put a plate of sliced sweet pears on the table by my bed. She smoothed my hair and kissed my cheek.

I ate the pears and I went to sleep, dreaming of a village at the North Pole.

The next day at school my teacher read us another story about a tall Christmas tree decorated with beautiful colored lights. How would Mr. Santa Claus ever find my dark house without colored lights to show him the way?

My teacher showed us how to make popcorn balls. She took us outside to hang them in the trees as presents for the birds. Then I had a very good idea, and I hid my popcorn ball in my pocket.

When I got home from school, I hung my popcorn present in the bush by our big window. Then I took some bits of bread from our kitchen and decorated the rest of the bushes.

The birds would be so happy. They would eat the treats and fly, fly away to the North Pole. They would sing a song for Santa Claus. They would tell him where to find me. "Little Yoon is here! She is here in America!"

When my mother went into the front room, she screamed. "Eeee!"

"What? What?" my father said as we both hurried to see what was the matter.

"Look! Look! There are so many birds! They are attacking our bushes!" she said.

There were big birds and little birds and blue birds and brown birds. They were pecking at our bushes and flying off with the bits of bread.

I clapped my hands and laughed. "My Christmas bushes," I said. "Presents for the birds."

My father scowled at me.

A large gray squirrel leaped into the biggest bush and stared at us.

"EEEE!" my mother screamed again. She jumped backwards.

Then the squirrel grabbed my popcorn ball and dashed away with it.

At school the boys and girls talked about the stockings they would hang on Christmas Eve. Mr. Santa Claus would fill them with surprises. I knew my mother and father would not allow me to hang a Christmas stocking.

After school I found my mother embroidering. "We will take this gift when we visit Mrs. Kim on New Year's Day. Do you think this is pretty?" my mother asked. She held up the lotus flower on the corner of the new tablecloth.

"Yes, Mother. Pretty," I said. "I learned a pretty song in school today. It is about a reindeer with a red nose. This reindeer is Santa Claus's favorite."

My mother shook her head. "Yoon," she said, "your father and I have told you we are not a Christmas family. We are a Korean family. Now dry your tears."

If only my mother and father could hear the stories and sing the songs!

Before I climbed into bed that night, I pinned my most colorful mitten to the bottom corner of my blanket. It would be my Christmas mitten. Santa Claus would come and leave a present.

My mother came to tuck me in. "What is this?" she asked.

"Please, Mother. Please let me keep it there," I begged. "It is my Christmas mitten."

My mother sighed. After she left, I heard my father and mother whispering in the front room.

When my father came in to see me, he asked, "What is this I hear about a Christmas mitten?"

I lowered my eyes. "When Santa Claus comes, that is where he will leave my surprise."

My father shook his head. "Yoon, I have told you. It is not the Korean way."

"But, Father," I said, "you have also told me that America is our home now. Are we not both Korean and American?"

My father sat quietly for a few moments. Then he nodded. "You are full of shining wisdom, little Yoon. We have named you well. You have given me something to think about." He patted my head and wished me a good night.

On Christmas Eve I lay in my bed, looking out at the starless sky. Wispy clouds covered the moon. How would Santa Claus ever find his way?

Maybe if I sang a Christmas song, Mr. Santa Claus would hear me. "Aha!" he would say. "Here is that little girl named Yoon!"

So I hummed quietly. I hummed the song about the reindeer with the red nose. Then I remembered my school friends said Santa Claus would not come until I fell asleep. I closed my eyes and I wished and I waited.

Sometime later I awoke. I heard the floor creak, and I peeked out from under my blankets. A shadow figure crept to my bed. The shadow figure carried a big box and laid it on the floor.

My heart danced. It must be Santa Claus! It *is* Santa Claus!

After Santa Claus left, I wanted to jump out of bed to see what he had brought me. But suddenly the shadow returned and reached for my Christmas mitten. I squeezed my eyes shut.

When it seemed like a long, long time had passed, I crawled out of bed and slipped my hand into the mitten. Yes! There was something inside! But what was it? I went to the window to look at my present in the dim moonlight. Was it a folded fan? A pencil? I would have to wait until morning to find out.

"Look! Look in the box!" I said to my father and mother. "Mr. Santa Claus brought me a new red dress! A dress that does not pinch or pop!"

"Well!" my father said, smiling at my mother.

"And look!" I said. I showed them the red-and-white stick I had found in my mitten. "Mr. Santa Claus brought me a piece of the North Pole!"

"Well!" my mother said, smiling at my father.

When I returned to school after the holiday vacation, I wore my new red dress. I told my teacher and the boys and girls all about our New Year's celebration. I told them about our fine dinner with *kimchee,* our spicy cabbage, and about the dumpling soup and the rice cakes. I told them about the good-luck wishes. Then I showed them the piece of the North Pole that Mr. Santa Claus had brought me.

"That is not the North Pole," the freckle boy said.

"That is peppermint candy. You should eat it."

"Eat it? I could never eat it. No, no, no." I shook my head.

"Eat it! Yes!" the children said.

My teacher smiled. "Try it," she said.

All eyes were looking at me.

"Well . . . maybe I could take a tiny taste." I unwrapped the red-and-white stripes, and I took a little lick. I smiled. I tasted the magic of Christmas, and it was sweet.

To my husband, Michael, my Santa Claus
—H.R.

To Michal and Lidia
—G.S.

Text copyright © 2006 by Helen Recorvits
Illustrations copyright © 2006 by Gabi Swiatkowska
All rights reserved
Distributed in Canada by Douglas & McIntyre Ltd.
Color separations by Chroma Graphics PTE Ltd.
Printed and bound in the United States of America by Phoenix Color Corporation
Designed by Jay Colvin
First edition, 2006
1 3 5 7 9 10 8 6 4 2

www.fsgkidsbooks.com

Library of Congress Cataloging-in-Publication Data
Recorvits, Helen.
   Yoon and the Christmas mitten / Helen Recorvits ; pictures by Gabi
Swiatkowska.— 1st ed.
      p.   cm.
   Summary: Yoon, a Korean American, is excited to hear about Santa Claus and
Christmas at her school, but her family tells her that such things are not part of
their Korean tradition.
   ISBN-13: 978-0-374-38688-7
   ISBN-10: 0-374-38688-9
   1. Korean Americans—Juvenile fiction.   [1. Korean Americans—Fiction.
2. Immigrants—Fiction.   3. Christmas—Fiction.]   I. Swiatkowska, Gabriela, ill.
II. Title.

PZ7.R24435 Yoo 2006
[E]—dc22
                                                                    2005045069